WHERE ARE THE WORDS

Jodi McKay

pictures by
Denise Holmes

Albert Whitman & Company
Chicago, Illinois

To my favorite, my Riley—JM

To Renee, who is always there to help me find the words—DH

Library of Congress Cataloging-in-Publication data is on file with the publisher.

Text copyright © 2016 by Jodi McKay
Pictures copyright © 2016 by Albert Whitman & Company
Pictures by Denise Holmes
Published in 2016 by Albert Whitman & Company
ISBN 978-0-8075-8733-1

Printed in China
10 9 8 7 6 5 4 3 2 1 LP 24 23 22 21 20 19 18 17 16

Design by Jordan Kost

For more information about Albert Whitman & Company,
visit our web site at www.albertwhitman.com.

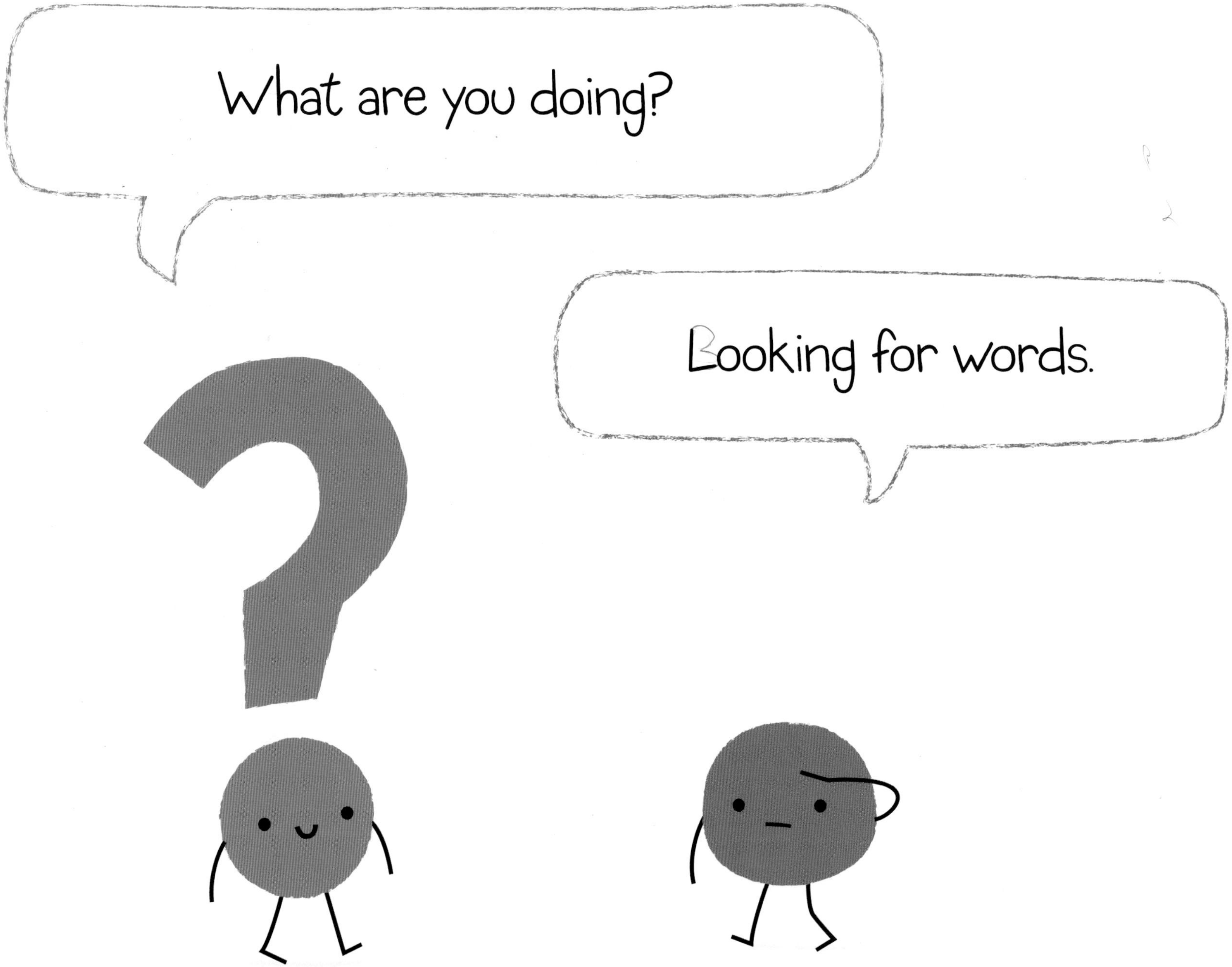
What are you doing?
Looking for words.

The wizard felt like giving up, but his friends wouldn't let him.

"A long time ago, in a galaxy far, far away…" A wizard had two problems: his magic words had vanished, and he was out of peanuts. He looked high and low (he may have looked left and right too), but still, no words.

"Will I ever find them?" he asked. The wizard felt like giving up, but his friends wouldn't let him.

What now?

Here we go again.